Bella and Ste
Visit the Fire Station!

MW01595540

Written by Tina Hawkins

Illustrated by Jeanette Hawkins

Bella and Stella Visit the Fire Station
Copyright © 2018 by Tina Hawkins

All rights reserved.
SBH LLC

This book may not be reproduced in whole or in part without permission from the author or illustrator; nor may any part of this book be reproduced, stored in a retrieval system or transmitted in any form or by means, electronic, mechanical, photocopying, recording or any other, without written permission from the author/publisher, or illustrator.

ISBN: 978-069208051-1

Dedicated to our past, present, and future pets that provide unconditional love and happiness in our lives.

A portion of all proceeds will be donated to organizations that focus on the well-being and rescue of animals.

Bella   Stella

In memory of a dear friend and fireman who fought more than one hard battle.

Hello! My name is Bella,
and this is my friend Stella.

We are going to the
fire station you see, so come on
along with Stella and me.

5

When at the fire station whom do we meet?
Fireman Kirk and Fireman Pete!

They give us a hat
all shiny and red.

Stella smiles proudly
when placed on her head.

We see the red trucks
all parked in a row.

Ready and waiting
for the siren to blow!

Then Fireman Bill
shows us a rule.

We look and we listen
like we were in school.

13

We practice the rule.
Stop, Drop, and Roll.

Stella keeps rolling
right into a pole!

I help Stella up
and I brush off her hat.

Fireman Tom gives us
both a nice pat.

We go into the kitchen
for a bite to eat.

Stella likes the bones,
and I love the meat.

When all of a sudden
there's a really loud beep!

Stella swallows her bone,
and I jump out of my seat.

The firemen pull on their boots
and put on their hats.

There isn't a minute to spare,
they have to move fast.

We climb up on the truck
all the way to the top.

I tell Stella, "Hold on
'til we come to a stop."

They pull out their hoses
and get ready to aim.

We watch with excitement
as they put out the flames.

Now back to the station
in case another call comes.

We know the Firemen will be
ready if and when it does.

We say "Thank you," to Firemen
Tom, Bill, and Kirk

for the excitng adventure
and showing us how they work.

We receive the Bone of Honor
from Fireman Pete.

Say, "Goodbye," to our friends,
and walk with pride down the street.

Bella and Stella have taken many adventures.

Be sure to read all about them!

Coming Soon!

Bella and Stella Visit the Vet

Follow Bella and Stella in their real-life adventures at:

www.bellaandstellaadventures.com